Plea Of The Damned 2
Forgive Me Aiden

Plea Of The Damned 2
Forgive Me Aiden

Avril Sabine

Cracked Acorn Productions
Australia

Plea Of The Damned 2: Forgive Me Aiden

Published by

Cracked Acorn Productions

PO Box 1365

Gympie, Queensland 4570

Australia

978-1-925131-51-2 (Kindle)

978-1-925131-76-5 (EPUB)

978-1-925131-52-9 (Print)

Genre: Young Adult Urban Fantasy/Paranormal

Copyright 2015 © Avril Sabine

Cover design by Caitlyn Petersen

*Once again this is for all of you who have
ever made a mistake and wanted to take it
back the moment it was made.*

Plea Of The Damned

Have you ever done something and immediately wished you could undo it? Jack knows that feeling very well. He's damned, bound to haunt his old school and help students until he atones for his sins. It's the last thing he wants to do. But since the alternative is an eternity in hell, he's not about to say no.

Book 2: Forgive Me Aiden

Aiden has been waiting for years to live with his father again. He knows this time will be different. His father has promised it will be. But somehow things aren't turning out like he expected. The ghost he met can't be right. Things will improve. He just needs to figure out how to solve all the problems piling up before someone gets hurt.

*

This story was written by an Australian author using Australian spelling.

Chapter One

Jack

Jack Richards leaned against one of the buildings, watching the craziness of the last day of school, as everyone left for the Easter holidays. Even though he was unable to feel the temperature, his leather jacket was slung over one shoulder so that he wore only his white t-shirt and jeans. Several metres away he saw Lucy giving Jasmine a hug, laughing at something her friend said. When Jasmine squealed at Lucy's reply Jack winced, glad he was far enough away not to have to experience the full effect of that sound.

It had been a few weeks since he'd helped Lucy and he hadn't seen the angel once. Not even a glimpse. How was he meant to atone for all his sins if they didn't let him help anyone? Or maybe that was the plan.

He wouldn't be surprised if it was deliberate. Get his hopes up then make him wait for ages before they let him help anyone else. Why hadn't that blasted bird returned? He was pretty sure the angel was too perfect to do something as commonplace as forget about him. Any forgetting would be on purpose. Just like the supposed forty-nine years he was meant to have waited before he could start atoning for his sins. Leaving him wait longer was sure to have been deliberate. Had the angel apologised? No, of course not. That blasted bird had acted like it was his own fault. If he had anyone he could complain to, he probably would have. As it was, the only one he could complain to was the angel, who'd disregarded every single complaint he'd made last time.

He still couldn't believe they expected him to offer help and guidance. Setting him a task like that was almost like they were hoping he'd fail. Yeah, get the major screw up to help others. Good plan. He moved away from the wall, that he hadn't really been leaning against, and turned his back on the students leaving for the holidays. Some habits were hard to break and leaning against things, even when he couldn't actually touch anything, was one of them. Sliding his arms into his leather jacket, he strode in the direction of the groundsman's shed where he'd created his own little space. The sound of students was left behind and he didn't see any as he crossed the grounds. Not that he blamed them. Who'd want to hang around any longer than they had to on the day the holidays started?

Ahead of him he saw the stand of trees the groundsman's shed was nestled amongst. It wasn't much of a place, but it was out of the way and he'd managed to claim a section of the timber shed for himself.

It had taken ages to push the wardrobe away from the wall. The first time had taken several years. During those early years the groundsmen had kept pushing it back into place. Each time he'd pushed it away from the wall it had become easier. Now they left it alone. It had to have been at least a couple of decades since the groundsmen had tried to push the wardrobe against the wall. There'd been a lot of questions and accusations, but in the end they'd shrugged and accepted it as fact. The wardrobe wouldn't stay against the wall.

Even though he couldn't touch anything and could only sometimes move things and unlock doors through force of will, he'd still wanted his own space. Being stuck around people who couldn't see or hear you all the time got a bit too much. And it wasn't like he could leave the school grounds to get away from everyone. Which brought him back to his original thought. Why hadn't the angel told him about someone else who needed help? How long was he going to make him wait? It better not be years.

"Blasted bird," he muttered as he reached the groundsman's shed, which was locked. About to step straight through the door, a voice behind him had him turning around.

"Nice to see you being your usual cheery self. Have you considered that working on your attitude might make your days a little more bearable?"

Jack glared at the angel. What would he know? "You couldn't have come sooner? How am I meant to atone for my sins if you don't let me help anyone? Didn't you hear me call out several times that I wanted to know who I was to help next?"

"I heard. This school isn't filled with endless people in major trouble."

He hadn't thought of that. "You could have told me. Ignoring someone is bad manners. Don't angels have standards they have to live up to or something?" The blasted bird enjoyed making a fool of him. What would it have hurt for the angel to have popped in, said he'd be back when he found someone who needed help and that there was no one currently in need. He wasn't the only one who needed to work on his attitude.

"It sounds like you'll be happy to hear I have someone who needs help."

"Now? But they're all going on holidays." Typical. Give him an assignment and make him wait to complete it. "How am I meant to help anyone if they're not here?" Another thought occurred to him. "Or are you letting me leave the school grounds?" That'd be good. He could find his way around this place with his eyes closed. It'd be nice to have a break from it.

"No. He'll be here Saturday night. A possible future student. Depending on the choices he makes."

He tried to mask his disappointment and barely stopped himself from asking if he'd ever be allowed to leave the school grounds. "Why would someone come to a school at night." His eyes narrowed. "Unless they're up to no good."

"Ahh, the voice of experience talking."

Out of habit, Jack started to deny the accusation. He stopped before he'd uttered a sound. Angels probably weren't that easily fooled and he was pretty certain this angel knew all his past sins. The minor ones as well as the major ones. "Are you going to tell me his name? Or are you going to be more helpful than last time and actually tell me what needs doing, instead of making me guess?"

"Aiden."

"And that's it? No clues about what he needs help with? And is he meant to make decisions that'll make him a student or is he meant to avoid those choices?"

The angel slowly shook his head, making a sound of disapproval. "Are you still expecting me to do your job for you?"

"No, but-" He broke off, thinking about how difficult it had been trying to figure out what Lucy had needed help with. "Don't you want them to have a chance?"

"Of course I do, that's why you've been asked to help. The question is, do you want them to have a chance?" The angel gave Jack an angelic smile before he disappeared.

"Blasted bird." He turned and walked through the door of the groundsman's shed. It wouldn't have hurt the angel to have at least given him a hint about Aiden's problem. Was that too much to ask? And of course he wanted them to have a chance. Just because he'd screwed up his life, didn't mean he wanted other kids to do the same. Not that he wanted to help them either, but what choice did he have in the matter? He'd been assured he wouldn't like the alternative. He had no idea how bad hell was and he didn't want to find out.

Jack strode through the clutter in the groundsman's shed and to his area behind the wardrobe. At this time of day, although there was very little light coming into the shed, there was more than enough for him to see the picture on the wall. His annoyance at the angel faded as he came to a stop in front of it. Even though he couldn't touch anything, he reached out, his hand stopping millimetres away from the face of the girl in the picture. If he managed to atone for all his sins, would Rose forgive him?

She'd told him never, but there wasn't a day that went by that he didn't regret her death. How did you atone for that? He feared it wasn't possible. He dropped his hand to his side. If he could have taken it back, he would have. But some mistakes could never be fixed. He heard the sound of the gunshot echoing through his memories. It was a sound he could never forget.

Chapter Two

Aiden

Aiden lay on the mattress on the floor of the otherwise nearly empty bedroom, his hands behind his head as he stared at the stained ceiling. The only other contents in the room were his unpacked suitcase, which he was certain his grandmother had owned since the fifties, and a smallish black backpack. The beat of the music he listened to made the paper thin walls vibrate and he wished his father would turn it down. Normally he wouldn't have minded music this loud, but he wasn't into eighties heavy metal. He was surprised the upstairs neighbour hadn't banged on the floor again. The old man had probably given up since every other time he'd done it yesterday it hadn't changed a thing. Actually at one stage his father had turned the music up louder, to give the man 'something to really complain about'.

Feeling his phone vibrate, Aiden drew it from his pocket and checked who was calling. He nearly groaned. Could she have picked a worse time to ring? With how loud the music was it would be nearly impossible to convince his grandmother that her son was providing a suitable environment for him. Before he answered the call he climbed out the window of his bedroom and into the backyard that was shared by all the tenants in the block of six flats. Luckily his father was renting one of the three on the ground floor or he would have had to go out and ask if he could turn the music down again. The last time he'd done that, his father had suggested he not answer the call and his grandmother would eventually get the message and stop pestering him.

He headed for the unpainted paling fence that was half falling down, trying to avoid stepping on the large patches of prickles. As soon as he was far enough away from the music, he answered the call.

"Is everything okay?"

He tried not to sigh at the worry he could hear in her voice. She'd asked him that every time. "It's all good, Grandma." He'd only been here since five o'clock yesterday afternoon and she'd rung him four times, each time sounding more worried than the last. How was she going to be by the end of the school holidays? Or worse, how would she cope when he finally convinced her it was different this time, and he wanted to move in with his father. His mind shied away from memories of the last time he'd lived with him. Things were different now.

"Are you sure? I mean, I love Gary and all, but I know my son is far from perfect. You'd let me know if there was a problem, wouldn't you?"

"You can stop worrying. Dad and I talked for hours last night. You've got nothing to worry about." So many things made sense after that talk. Things he'd been too young to understand.

"Promise me you'll ring if you have a problem."

"Sure, Grandma." There wasn't going to be a problem. Why couldn't she understand that? He guessed it was to be expected since she hadn't been there last night and heard everything his father had said. "Quit worrying, okay?" He heard her sigh heavily and wished there was some way he could convince her she didn't have to worry.

"What have you been doing today?"

"Getting to know Dad again." Well, it was kind of true. He now knew he didn't think much of his father's taste in music. "I've got to go. Someone's trying to get my attention." They weren't exactly trying to get his attention. It was probably the opposite. The old man from upstairs looked like he thought no one could see him with the way he peered out around the edge of the curtain into the backyard. He wondered if the man planned to come outside and say something about the music.

"You make sure you ring if you need me."

"As long as you stop ringing me. I'll call you in the morning for Easter." When she agreed, he disconnected, slid his phone into a pocket of his jeans and headed back to his room. He took the same careful path through the prickles and climbed in the window. There wasn't a single screen in the entire flat, which meant the windows needed to be shut at dusk if you didn't want the place filled with mosquitoes during the night. He'd learned that the hard way and had spent at least an hour, last night, hunting them down before he could go to sleep. There was nothing worse than listening to their high-pitched whine in the dark. Although eighties heavy metal music turned up loud enough to make the walls vibrate had to come a close second.

Hearing the music being turned down, he decided to go talk to his father again. Maybe they could have another talk like they'd had last night. He couldn't wait to move in. They'd made so many plans throughout the night. All he had to do was convince his grandmother that moving in with his father was the best thing for him. He'd only opened the door a crack when he heard another voice. Not wanting to barge in, he stayed in place.

"It won't be for long."

He peered through the gap, feeling a little bit like the old man upstairs. A large man stood near his father in the open plan living area, which was really a fancy name for an overcrowded space that was meant to be kitchen, dining and lounge. The man was taller than his father, who was six foot one. But it wasn't the way the man loomed over Gary that made Aiden stay in his room. It was a combination of everything. The tattooed, muscular arms shown off by a singlet, a scruffy black beard, the way he stood as if ready for a fight, black jeans that had faded to charcoal and scuffed combat boots.

Chapter Three

Aiden

"I don't know, Phil. I've got the kid here," Gary said. "What if he sees them? I've still got things I need to talk to him about. This wasn't part of our agreement."

"So put the parcel in your room. He's not about to go snooping, is he? If he does, take your belt to him and he'll think twice before doing it again," Phil said.

Aiden was glad he'd stayed in his room. He reduced the size of the crack he looked through. What was his father doing hanging out with someone like that? Phil reminded him of the people who'd hung around the last time he'd lived with his father. Ten years ago when he was seven. Some of them had given him nightmares. Particularly the one who'd looked like he was from the horror movie he'd watched when he was five. His father had been sitting around drinking with a handful of mates and the television had been playing in the background. No one had sent him to bed so he'd continued to watch it, eventually letting them all know he was awake when he screamed. They'd teased him about it for months.

Gary chuckled. "I can't see myself doing that. The kid's nearly as tall as me now. Not even an inch separating us."

Was that pride he heard in his father's voice or was it only wishful thinking that had him hearing it? Why didn't his father tell Phil to go?

"I'll give you a grand for holding it."

"I don't know, Phil. You shouldn't even be visiting me or I could end up back behind bars. I thought you said you wouldn't come around here until they stopped watching me. You'll ruin everything."

"They have. No one's been spotted hanging around you for a few weeks. I'll give you a grand and a half. All you'll have to do is hold it for a couple of weeks. I have a buyer. I'm just waiting for him to meet me. He's currently out of town. All I need is somewhere safe to stash it until he returns."

"I don't know. Who's to say the deal will go through? It wouldn't be the first time one hasn't panned out."

Aiden wanted to rush out and tell his father not to give in. He didn't want to lose him for another ten years. Not after finally getting him back.

Phil drew out his wallet and took five crisp twenty-dollar notes from it. He held them up as he returned his wallet to his pocket, Gary's gaze following them. "I'll give you a hundred now and fifteen hundred after the deal goes through."

Aiden's heart sank. He could see it in his father's face that he wasn't about to turn Phil down. As he stared at him, he couldn't help searching for any similarities between them. He looked nothing like his father, with his stubble of brown hair and green eyes. Aiden kept his black hair short and his brown eyes came from the mother he'd never seen. Unless you counted the day she'd given birth to him, even though he'd been too young to remember the experience. The only thing he had in common with his father, as his grandmother sometimes pointed out, was his smile. According to her it was perfect for conmen, used car salesmen, politicians and dentists. She always followed it up by telling him she was sure he'd make a great dentist. That was the last thing he wanted to be. Not that he wanted to be any of the others.

Gary reached for the money. "Even if the deal falls

through, I still get to keep the hundred?" At Phil's nod, he shoved the money into his pocket. "Two weeks."

Phil nodded. "Three at the most."

"I could do with some cash."

"Who can't these days?" Phil drew a parcel from the leather satchel he had slung over one shoulder. The worn satchel looked like it should have been replaced several years ago.

Gary tried to take the parcel from Phil. "I'll stash it in my room. "

"I know exactly what's in here." Phil held onto the parcel until Gary nodded. "I'll be back to collect it when the buyer's ready. Let me know if you have any problems." He didn't stick around, leaving before Gary could do little more than nod again.

Aiden watched his father enter his own room, closing the door behind him. What was he going to do? His father had promised he'd changed. Promised that things would be different and there was no way he wanted to spend another day in jail. Ten years had been more than long enough. Aiden shut his door properly and leaned against it. It looked like those promises had a price. What was he going to do?

A knock on his door startled him and he turned to open it. His father stood there. "Yeah?"

"I've got to pop out to the shop for a bit. Won't be long. Do you need anything?"

How about that man from last night who'd promised him everything would be different? Like he could bring himself to say that to his father. He'd instantly know he'd been spying on him. "Nah. I'm right."

"I'll see you soon."

He waited until Gary had been gone for several minutes before he hurried into the bedroom, searching for the parcel. He found it on the top shelf of the wardrobe, some ratty sweaters shoved in front of it. Holding the parcel in his hands, he stared at it for a moment, trying to decide if he wanted to open it.

Anything could be in it. His father hadn't even asked Phil what he wanted him to look after. Unless that had been discussed before he'd started listening into the conversation. What if it was drugs? That would certainly put his father back in jail.

Eventually he gave in, needing to know what was going on. He carefully opened the parcel and stared at the contents. He closed his eyes, wishing he could open them to find he'd been imagining things. It didn't work. Opening his eyes he stared at the jewellery, all of it looking very real and very expensive. Phil hadn't looked like the kind of man who owned this type of jewellery. He pulled out a string of diamonds, gasping at the fortune he probably held. From the amount of jewellery store windows Karina, his girlfriend, had peered into longingly, he knew jewellery wasn't cheap. Dropping the necklace back into the parcel, he momentarily closed his eyes again. This wasn't going to end well. How could his father do this to him?

Returning the parcel to the wardrobe, he made sure it looked the same as it had before he'd touched it. What was he going to do? He should probably return to his own room before his father came home and found him snooping. There had to be something he could do.

Standing in his own room, he stared at the mattress on his floor. His father had promised to take him shopping for furniture next week, once all the Easter madness was over. Would that be another promise he'd break? He stood for several minutes in his room, feeling lost. He didn't want to believe his grandmother could be right to be so worried. All he wanted was the chance to get to know his father. Surely that wasn't too much to ask.

Chapter Four

Aiden

By the time Gary returned, Aiden was in the living area sprawled on the lounge chair staring at the television. It didn't help. He might as well have been staring at a blank screen for all the attention he'd given it. He watched as his father carried in a carton of beer and took a can out, putting the rest in the fridge.

Gary held up the can. "Want a drink?"

Aiden shook his head, worried that if he spoke he'd demand to know what was going on.

Gary swung the fridge door shut. "You've been living with my mum too long. I would've jumped at the chance of a beer when I was your age."

He shrugged. It wasn't that he disliked beer. He

probably would've jumped at the offer if it had come before Phil's visit.

Gary sat in one of the single armchairs, opening the can. "What's up with you? Couldn't shut you up last night and now I can't get a word out of you."

"Nothing." Was fifteen hundred worth the risk of returning to jail? It was an effort to keep the words from tumbling out.

"Yeah well, whatever you're sulking about, get over it." Gary looked at the television. "What's this crap? Where's the remote?"

Aiden held out the remote that had been on the floor in front of him.

"Toss it over."

Aiden threw the remote to his father. Gary remained silent and Aiden struggled to think of something to say. In the end, he gave up. There was no way he could start a conversation without demanding to know what his father was doing. Gary had been out of jail for six months and this was the first time he'd been able to spend more than a few hours with him. His grandmother hadn't let him stay overnight until his father had found his own place to rent. Although she'd been fairly critical of the place when she'd seen it.

When his phone vibrated from an incoming call,

Aiden used it as an excuse to leave the room. Seeing it was Karina, he was even more relieved he'd chosen to leave the living room. There was no way he wanted to talk to his girlfriend in front of his father.

"Missing me yet?"

He smiled at her familiar greeting. "Absolutely." He dropped onto the mattress and lay back, putting one arm under his head to pillow it, staring at the ceiling again. With the amount of time he'd spent looking at it today he could probably draw an image of all the stains without referring to the ceiling once.

"Then why don't you come and see me. Couldn't you have gone to your dad's place a day or two later?"

It was nearly an hour's drive to the suburb his grandmother and all his friends lived in. Not that he had his own car, although he did have a license. "I'll catch a bus over next week and spend the day with you."

"One day out of the entire school holidays?"

"I'll come over a couple of times."

"That's hardly any time at all. If you end up moving in with your dad I'll see even less of you. Why would you want to move so far away? Changing schools partway through year twelve is crazy."

"Nothing's been decided yet." Nothing would be

decided if his grandmother had her way. He tried to push the problem of the jewellery from his mind, but it was impossible.

"I could get my mum to drop me over there one day early next week."

"No, it's okay. I can come to your place." If his grandmother had been critical of his father's flat, that was nothing compared to how Karina's mother would feel about it.

They talked for nearly an hour and Aiden told Karina he needed to go when he heard a knock at the front door. Worried it was Phil returning, he opened his door slightly. He couldn't see who it was because his father hadn't opened the door properly. It took him several minutes to work out what was going on from listening to the conversation. His heart raced and, panicked, he grabbed his backpack and joggers, slipping into his father's room.

Over and over again he kept telling himself what he was doing was crazy. But he couldn't help it. He couldn't lose his father for another ten years. Grabbing the parcel, he shoved it in his backpack and climbed out his father's window and into the backyard. Putting his shoes on, he glanced around, finding the area empty. Not wanting to be spotted by anyone who might be out the front, he strode to the paling fence. He wasn't even halfway there before a voice calling out made him freeze, his heart pounding even faster.

"Oi!"

Fighting the urge to run, he slowly turned and saw the old man standing on the upstairs landing. He didn't have time for this, whatever this was. His gaze darted around the backyard. They were alone.

"Do you think you can manage not to have your music going all night, tonight?"

He opened his mouth to argue against the man's comment, but didn't get a chance to speak.

"Some people like to sleep, you know. It's rude having it playing all hours of the night and day."

It looked like interrupting was the only way he'd be able to say his piece. "You'll have to talk to my dad about that. It's his music, not mine." He continued towards the fence, ignoring the old man's complaints about disrespectful teenagers. He didn't have time to stand around arguing. It was unfair the old man had instantly blamed him.

With a last glance over his shoulder, he pushed his way through one of the gaps. Had Phil set his father up, or had someone else told the authorities about Phil's visit? He was several blocks away before it occurred to him that taking the parcel to protect his father had made him an accessory. His steps slowed.

The school holidays had barely begun and already they were turning into a disaster. Ringing his grandmother was out of the question. She'd tell him to go to the police. He knew it was the right thing to do. He wasn't an idiot. Okay, so maybe he was, but he really wanted the chance to get to know his father. Surely his father deserved the opportunity to sort his life out. He remembered all the regrets his father had spoken of last night. He wanted him to have a chance to fix some of them. Particularly the one about wanting to do some father-son things, like fishing. He wasn't so sure he'd enjoy fishing, but if it gave him some time with his father he was willing to give it a try.

Looking around, he tried to figure out where he could go on a Saturday afternoon while carrying a fortune in jewellery. It'd be night soon and this didn't look like the sort of neighbourhood to be wandering around after dark, with something worth stealing. He picked up his pace, his gaze drawn to every sound. Seeing a man on the other side of the road, he lengthened his stride, even though he had no destination in mind.

There was a couple of mates he could call, who

either owned a vehicle or had access to one, but it'd still take them at least an hour to get to him. Every plan he came up with, he thought of a flaw. Eventually his surroundings started to improve and by the time the sun had set he was across the road from a school. Following the fence line, he found a well treed corner and jumped the fence. He felt a little better now he wasn't out in the open. Even though it was dark, there were more than enough streetlights for someone to have spotted him.

He tried to see into the darkness beneath the stand of trees. The place should be deserted during the school holidays. If he hid the parcel under one of the trees no one should stumble across it. Hopefully the dirt under the trees would be soft enough to dig by hand. Using the screen of his phone to light his way, he chose a tree with plenty of leaf litter under it and a distinctive branch he should recognise when he needed to find the parcel again. Sliding his phone into his pocket he started to crouch at the base of the tree. The sooner he could ditch the parcel, the better. Then he'd stop feeling like every shadow was about to attack him.

Chapter Five

Aiden

"What are you doing?"

Heart racing, Aiden spun to see a shadowy figure standing not far from him. He should have been able to hear the man walking through the leaf litter. It should have been impossible for anyone to sneak up on him. Taking a step back, he ran into the tree. "How did you get here?"

"I guess you could say I'm always here."

"No, how did you get so close without me hearing you?"

The man laughed.

Aiden guessed it was time to go. Obviously this wasn't a place he could hide the parcel. He stepped around the tree, wanting to put some distance between him and the stranger. Reaching for his phone, he shone the light of the screen on the ground. He didn't want to trip over anything on his way to the fence.

"Aiden, wait."

He spun to face the man, shining the light of his screen on him. Before the light dimmed he saw someone about his own age dressed up to look like he was from the late fifties or early sixties, including wearing a black leather jacket. "Who are you?" Fear raced through him. Was it someone Phil had sent after him? How would he have known where he went? He hadn't even known where he was going. Surely the stranger hadn't followed him the entire way. Who else was hiding in the shadows? He used the screen light to check the area.

The stranger held out a hand. "I'm Jack Richards."

Aiden took a step back. There was no way he was getting that close. "Who do you think you are? That dude from the old TV show who wears a leather jacket and rides a motorbike?" He couldn't think of the character's name, but he remembered looking the show up on Youtube a couple of years ago when his grandmother had said she missed shows like that. He'd queued a few of them up on his laptop for her to watch and she'd convinced him to join her.

"Look, I know this is going to sound odd, but I

know you're in some kind of trouble and I want to help you."

He didn't believe a word Jack said. There was no way some random stranger would offer help when he was carrying a fortune in jewellery if he didn't know about them. It was too much of a coincidence. Spinning, he raced through the trees, using his phone to light his way. Jack must somehow know he had the jewellery. Nothing else made sense. He could see the fence ahead of him. He forced himself to run faster. A body collided with him, causing him to crash to the ground. The phone flew from his hands and he dropped his backpack, struggling to get away. Curling his hand into a fist, he struck out at Jack. He wasn't about to let him get the jewellery.

It was nearly impossible to fight in the dark. He felt like he was fighting shadows. Somehow Jack pinned him to the ground within minutes. He had no idea where his backpack or phone was. "Let me go. Who sent you? Phil?" He struggled to break free.

"I wouldn't have a clue who Phil is, but if you stop trying to make tracks I'll explain everything."

Aiden stilled. "All right. Let me up and I'll listen." The moment he had his backpack and phone he was out of here. Not that he had anywhere to go.

Jack chuckled. "You know I don't think I will. I

reckon you'll cut out of here the moment I let you up."

"I hadn't planned to." No, he'd planned to find his gear first.

"This is going to sound a little off the wall, but here's the deal. I died in 1963 on my eighteenth birthday. My girlfriend stabbed me. Not that I blame her since I accidentally shot her. Although she did stab me before I shot her. But enough of that. An angel gives me the name of someone who needs help and by helping them, I manage to atone for one of my sins. This time it happens to be you."

If he wasn't so focused on trying to figure a way out of this mess, he'd laugh. "Nice try. Now let me up and tell me what's really going on. You know Phil, don't you?"

"I'll let you up, but we're going to walk over to the fence and I'm going to prove I'm a ghost."

"Sure." Now if only Jack would give him the chance to get his gear first. He wasn't about to stick around any longer than he had to. The moment Jack released him, he tried to find his backpack.

Jack grabbed his arm and pulled him up. "Leave it for now."

"I'm not about to leave my stuff for anyone to

come along and pick it up." Not with a fortune in jewellery in his backpack.

"No one else is around here. It's only you and me." Jack drew him towards the fence. "Come on."

Aiden had little choice. He couldn't outrun Jack or fight him in the dark. Maybe once they were over by the fence, where he could actually see what he was doing, he'd have a chance.

Reaching the dim light by the fence, Jack took hold of Aiden's hand, letting go of his arm. "Pay attention."

"What am I meant to be paying attention to?" His mouth dropped open when Jack's hand, that had been firmly holding his as if about to shake it in greeting, became as solid as mist. He reached out and pushed his hand through Jack's shoulder. He wasn't there. He could see him, but he couldn't feel him. He was tempted to run. Without his phone or backpack.

Jack took a step back. "Was that enough proof?"

Aiden slowly reached out to touch Jack's shoulder again. This time his hand landed on the leather jacket. He instantly drew it back. "How did you do that?" Ghosts weren't possible. There had to be a logical explanation.

"I told you. I'm a ghost."

Shaking his head, Aiden looked around. "It has to be some kind of trick. How did you do it?"

"Why is it so hard for people to believe in ghosts?"

"Probably because they don't exist." He tapped Jack's shoulder. It was still solid. "Can you do it again? What if we move to a different spot? Or can you only do it here? Is this where you've set up your trick?" He glanced around, trying to spot what Jack must have used to do the trick.

Jack sighed. "Is that what it'll take to convince you? I stop being solid in another location?"

Aiden shrugged. "Maybe. Let me grab my gear first." He walked cautiously back to where Jack had tackled him. "Can you glow in the dark? Isn't that meant to be something ghosts can do? Because that'd be really handy right now." He alternated between wanting to figure out Jack's trick and wanting to run.

"Your backpack is over here and your phone not far from it."

He followed Jack's voice. "If you can see them why don't you give them to me?" His foot ran into the bag.

"I can't pick anything up."

"Why not? You're solid, aren't you?" He checked his backpack before he swung it onto his shoulder. It was still closed. The jewellery should be safely inside. He wasn't about to check in front of Jack.

"Your phone is here." Jack paused. "I'm not exactly solid to anyone, or anything else, other than you."

He started to comment on that remark, but decided he'd be able to prove Jack wasn't real soon enough. Or maybe that should be that he was real. There was no such thing as a ghost. Finding his phone, he dusted it off and shone the screen light towards Jack. "All right, let's go somewhere else."

"Lead the way." Jack gestured towards the school buildings.

Aiden shook his head, pointing to the fence. "Out there, well away from here."

"I can't leave the school grounds."

Aiden stared at him for several seconds. Was the entire school grounds rigged for his trick? Surely not. That was a pretty big area from what he'd seen. "Okay. This way." He headed for the nearest light. When he reached it, he turned to Jack. "Prove it."

Jack held out his hand.

Chapter Six

Aiden

Aiden hesitated a moment before he took Jack's hand. Like before, it was first solid and then like mist. He drew back. It couldn't be real. He glanced around, spotting an area with more light. "This way."

Jack strode beside him. "How many times will it take to convince you?"

Aiden shrugged. He supposed that depended on how long it took him to figure out the trick. After four more times, he began to think it wasn't a trick. By the fifth time, he was almost certain it wasn't one. He stared at Jack, trying to make sense of the situation. "Why me?"

"What do you mean?"

"Why was I the one chosen for you to help?" There

was nothing special about him. Why would some stranger care what happened to him?

"I don't know. He never tells me anything."

"Who doesn't?"

"The angel."

A sense of unreality washed over him. Last night he'd thought these holidays were going to be perfect. All his dreams were about to come true. He'd finally get to be with his father again. Something he'd wanted since he was seven years old. Tonight he didn't know what was real anymore. "So what are you meant to do?"

Jack shrugged. "Help you sort out your problems."

"That would have to be my dad. He said he's changed, but the very next day he's getting involved with something that could put him straight back in jail."

Jack laughed, no humour evident in the sound. "I'm the last person you want advice from about fathers. By the time I died, I'd stopped talking to mine. It seemed easier than lying to him."

"Then how are you meant to help?"

"I've got a feeling it isn't by helping you fix your father. Come on." Jack strode back towards the trees.

Aiden watched him for a moment before hurrying after him. It didn't take him long to catch up with

Jack. "Where are we going?" He continued to use the light of the phone's screen to find his way.

"My place." Jack grinned. "It's not much of a place, but at least we'll be undisturbed if anyone else decides to wander through the school grounds tonight."

When they reached the stand of trees, where Jack had found him, Jack walked through the door of a shed and it flew open. "That ability looks like it might come in handy." He thought of his father and Phil. "For some."

"It doesn't always work. Shut the door behind you so no one thinks they can wander on in."

Closing the door, he shone the light over the clutter. There seemed to be a lot of gardening tools as well as some broken furniture. "What is this place?"

"The groundsman's shed. Come on. What's taking you so long?" Jack stepped through a wardrobe in the far corner.

Aiden tried to ignore how the sight of Jack walking through the wardrobe made him feel. It wasn't pleasant. He wound his way through everything. "Some of us can't walk through things." Not that he wanted to. It seemed like that ability only came with being dead. That was the last thing he wanted. Reaching the wardrobe, he had to push it a little further away from the wall to be able to slip behind it. His light fell on a picture stuck to the wall. "Who's the girl?"

"Rose." Jack stared at the picture for half a minute before he spoke again. "She was my girlfriend a long time ago." Jack faced Aiden, gesturing towards the floor. "It's nothing fancy, but at least we'll be undisturbed."

Aiden sat on the floor, leaning back against the wall and leaving his legs stretched out in front of him. There was just enough space. "What now?"

Jack sat down. He left one leg stretched out and drew the other up to rest his arm on his knee. "You tell me your problem so we can figure out how to fix it."

"I don't know where to start."

"Starting at the beginning usually makes the most sense."

Aiden glared at Jack, not liking his mocking tone. "Obviously." He didn't bother keeping the sarcasm from his voice. If Jack could be mocking, he could be sarcastic. It wasn't like he'd asked for Jack's help. The ghost had volunteered. "What I don't know is if I should start with my dad getting out of jail six months ago and wanting me to live with him or if I should go back to the very beginning of how he ended up in jail when I was seven years old and I had to live with my grandma."

"What about your mother? Why don't you live with her?"

"Because the one and only time she's ever seen me was the day she gave birth to me. Apparently I was a mistake she didn't want to put up with so she ditched both me and my dad."

"That's rough."

"Yeah." He fell silent as he thought of the handful of photos his grandmother had of his mother. She'd looked so young. "I can't blame her. She was a kid, really. Only sixteen." A year younger than him. "Dad wasn't much older, but he had Grandma to help him with me." Silence fell again. "Her name is Heidi. Her mum named her for some character in a book. She was living with an aunt when she met my dad. Grandma said she was grieving because she'd recently lost both her parents." He fell silent again. "But that was years ago. You wouldn't think she'd still be grieving." He'd never told anyone before, but somehow telling it to a ghost didn't feel like it counted. Although he still felt uncomfortable for having told Jack so much. He reached for his backpack and took out the parcel, opening it up.

"Twitchin."

He had no idea what the word meant, but from Jack's tone of voice, he sounded pretty amazed, possibly even admiring. "It's not exactly a little problem." He lifted out a gold necklace that had a large opal pendant hanging from it. "Not little at all."

"Who'd you rip them off?"

He continued to shine the light from his phone screen onto the jewellery. "My dad. I wasn't exactly stealing them from him, I was kind of trying to stop him from ending up back in jail."

"It sounds like you should tell me the entire story so we can figure out what to do."

Aidan nodded, this time leaving the light of his screen off when it faded. He started with his father getting out of jail six months ago, on parole. He talked about the arguments between his father and grandmother, who'd refused to let him live with his father until he had his own place. When Gary had found a flat she'd been cautious about letting him stay there because she hadn't liked the neighbourhood or the condition of the building. It had taken a lot of pleading to get her to agree that he could stay for the school holidays.

Talking about the long conversation between him and his father Friday night had been far more difficult than telling Jack his mother had abandoned him as a baby. By the time Aiden had told Jack about Phil and running with the jewellery, he was surprised to find it was nearly midnight.

Chapter Seven

Aiden

Aiden stared at the time on his phone. He'd said a lot more than he'd initially planned to.

"I don't usually think it's a good idea to rat on someone, but I think you should call the fuzz."

He dragged his gaze away from his phone and glared at Jack. "No. My dad will end up back in jail. I can't let that happen. Dad wants me to live with him." He'd been waiting for this moment for ages.

"Why?"

The light of the screen faded again and he touched it to make it brighten. "What do you mean why? He's my dad." He was tempted to get up and walk out. How dare Jack insinuate that neither of his parents were interested in having him in their lives.

"When I was younger and had got into trouble

for the same thing a second time, I told my mum I wouldn't do it again because I knew that's what she wanted to hear."

"What's that got to do with anything?"

"She looked me in the eye and told me she really wanted to believe me, but actions speak far louder than words. Anyone can speak any number of words, but it takes a great man to live up to them." Jack paused. "I wish I'd remembered that after she'd died."

"This is different. He does want me to live with him. We spoke about it for hours." He glared at Jack, not bothering to brighten the phone screen when the light faded and went out. Jack obviously had no idea what he was talking about.

"If you don't want to rat on them, what do you plan to do?"

"I don't know. I can't take the parcel back to my dad's place. What if it's discovered there?" He had no idea what the jewellery was worth, but it wouldn't surprise him if it was worth more than his grandmother's house.

"So you're going to hide it until Phil wants it back?"

That sounded worse. He'd definitely be an accessory if he did that. There had to be another option. "A great lot of help you're being."

"It's not my problem if you don't like my suggestions."

Aiden sighed. He had to go home sooner or later. "Can I leave the parcel here? Will anyone find it?"

"There shouldn't be anyone on the school grounds during these holidays. But that didn't stop you from being here. I can't guarantee no one will find it and if someone did I wouldn't be able to stop them from taking it."

He didn't have much choice. Like he'd already said, he couldn't take it back to his father's flat. He used the light from his screen to check the area for hiding places. The timber at the back of the wardrobe didn't go all the way to the floor like it did at the front and sides. It created a dark area underneath. The parcel fit, barely. He pushed it as far under as it would go. Hopefully no one would find it. Rising to his feet, he stared at Jack, trying to figure out what to say. "Thanks."

"What for?"

He shrugged, half smiling. "Trying. I guess it's not your fault you don't understand what's going on. I mean, you died decades ago. Things were different then."

"Not as much as you think."

Aiden shrugged again, not bothering to argue. Jack

didn't understand the situation. "I'll be back for the parcel." He squeezed between the wardrobe and the wall, making his way carefully through the clutter. Stepping outside, he closed the door behind him. A pity he didn't have a car. With a mental shrug, he strode for the fence and vaulted over it.

He stood on the footpath trying to figure out which direction to go in. He had a vague idea, but in the end he used an app on his phone to find out where he was and the streets he needed to take to return to his father's flat. Staring at the map on the screen of his phone, he was surprised at the distance he'd travelled. Returning his phone to his pocket, he straightened his shoulders and strode down the street.

The night was fairly quiet. He could hear vehicles in the distance and the occasional dog barking, but the streets he travelled were empty. Even the houses he passed were silent and dark. As the neighbourhood changed, so did the noise level. More houses had lights on and he saw a handful of people out and about. Luckily they were on the other side of the street and he didn't have to decide if he should walk past them or cross over. There were a few houses where parties seemed to be winding down and one party that sounded like it would continue for hours. He felt a twinge of regret that he'd knocked back taking Karina to a party one of their friends was having tonight. He wondered if it was finished yet or still going.

It was nearly two a.m. when he tried to open the door of his father's flat. It was locked and he didn't have a key. Seeing the light was still on, he knocked. The door swung open and Gary dragged him inside by the front of his shirt, kicking the front door shut. Shock momentarily kept him quiet and unmoving.

Gary slammed him up against the wall. "Where are they, you little punk?"

He tried to pull away from his father, surprised by the anger in his voice. Even though they were a similar height, his father was stronger than him. A touch of fear crept in at the look in his father's eyes.

"Well?" Gary refused to let him go. "You better not have pawned them."

Aiden could only stare at his father, memories of other times when he'd been in trouble flashing through his mind. He felt seven-years-old again. Small and defenceless.

"Are they in here?" Gary let him go to grab hold of the backpack. Pulling it open, he tipped the contents onto the floor, letting the empty bag fall on top of the scattered items.

Aiden stumbled forward and crouched on the floor,

shoving his gear into his backpack. Shock slowly turned into anger. He couldn't believe his father was treating him like this. He was no longer seven-years-old.

"Leave the kid be. I'm sure he was only trying to help." Phil patted the space on the lounge chair beside him. "Why don't you sit down and tell me where you've hidden the parcel."

Rising to his feet, Aidan slung his backpack over his shoulder, trying to ignore the fear that had raced through him at Phil's voice. He hadn't noticed him. He would have thought a man that size would have been hard to miss, but he guessed his attention had been taken up by his father. He glanced towards Gary, not sure what to do.

"I'm not gunna bite." Phil grinned.

He hoped that smile wasn't meant to be reassuring because it made him want to bolt for the door.

"If you've pawned them…" Gary let the threat hang in the air.

Aiden shook his head.

"There, see?" Phil looked towards Gary. "The kid was only helping. He didn't want his old man to get in trouble." Phil returned his gaze to Aiden. "Where did you leave them? It better be somewhere safe."

Even with how mild Phil's tone was, Aiden

recognised a threat when he heard it. He didn't care about a heap of jewellery. He wanted to erase this day and start again from last night. After talking to his father all night, he'd had so many expectations for the rest of the year. And even for the years after that. Surely it hadn't all been lies.

When Aiden remained silent, Phil's smile faded and he stood up. "You don't want to mess with me, kid. Where's my parcel?"

Hearing Phil's mild tone replaced by a snarl, Aiden looked towards Gary, who remained silent. He'd half expected his father to defend him. Instead, Gary's hard, angry expression brought to mind the words Jack had spoken. He hadn't wanted to believe, but Jack's mother was right. Actions did speak louder than words. He took a step away.

Phil took a step towards him, his gaze narrowing. "I don't like to repeat myself. Ask anyone, they'll tell you the same. Last chance. Where's my parcel?"

Chapter Eight

Aiden

Aiden didn't know what to do, so he did what he should have done the moment he'd first had the urge. He bolted out the door. Behind him he heard swearing, quickly followed by the sound of running footsteps. So much for telling his grandmother everything was okay. He was obviously not only an idiot, but clueless. He ran along the footpath, the sound of his feet loud against the hard packed dirt barely covered by grass. His father and Phil had finally stopped calling out to him, but they continued to follow. He forced his legs to go faster.

Why had his father asked him to move in with him? Nothing made sense. There hadn't been a single bit of caring in his father's expression when he'd stared at him. Only a warning that he wouldn't like what would happen next. Why did Gary want him to move in if he didn't care about him?

He couldn't worry about that right now. Not with Phil and Gary continuing to chase him. He didn't know about his father, but Phil looked like the sort to want revenge. After seeing the expression on his father's face, he had a bad feeling his father would feel the same way. Turning a corner, he glanced behind and seeing a tall, solid fence blocked him from view, ran through an open gate into the next yard. He hid under the steps of a high set house, crouching behind some shrubs. The block wall of the house was cold against his back, the sound of his heart beat loud in his ears. He tried to breathe quietly, not wanting anything to give him away.

He heard running feet go past the yard and held his breath as he waited for them to continue out of hearing. They stopped and turned around, coming back. Releasing his breath slowly, he remained pressed against the house. What were they doing? Had they noticed him after all?

"I could ring him," Gary said. "He can't be too far away. He's probably run through one of these yards."

"Don't ring him on your phone. It might be bugged. I thought you said your kid would do anything you told him to."

"I guess he's grown out of that hero worship stage. I could get him to do anything when he was a kid. He was turning into a right little conman. My mum's ruined him."

"We need to find another underage mule. We don't have much time left to organise everything."

"Sorry, Phil."

Aiden remained in place long after their voices had faded into the distance, even though the cold bricks at his back chilled his entire body. He was an idiot. No wonder his grandmother was so concerned and had kept ringing him until he'd told her not to. A clueless idiot. Even a ghost had known better than him. He rose to his feet, remaining hunched over until he was past the steps. What was he meant to do now? He didn't have a clue. Yep, a clueless idiot.

He strode to the gate and checked the street in both directions. Seeing no one, he broke into a run. He had nowhere to go. He thought of his grandmother. Okay, maybe not nowhere, but he needed to sort this problem out before he went home. He didn't want Phil anywhere near his grandmother. Or Gary. It sounded like his father wasn't that fond of her either. Did he care about anyone? After everything Gary had said last night he felt betrayed. He wished he'd never even considered moving in with him. He should have known better. As angry as he was with Gary, he was even angrier at himself.

Once he was several streets away, he slowed to a walk and used his app to figure out where he was. He sighed. It was going to take him ages to get back to the school. He stifled a yawn and continued down the street.

There was a hint of light in the sky by the time he arrived. He'd got lost a couple of times and had to use the app to check his direction. He came at the school from the main gate and seeing the name, realised it was the school he would've attended if he'd moved in with his father. His lips twisted into a smile at the irony of the situation. He followed the fence until he found the section that led to the treed area. Jack was waiting for him. He stood there silently, not sure what to say.

"If you're having trouble figuring out how to say something, it's usually easier to get it over and done with," Jack said.

"That's not it. Well, not exactly. It's more that there isn't anything to say." He vaulted the fence and gestured towards the groundsman's shed, not wanting to be out in the open. Jack led the way, vanishing through the door. After he'd opened the door, and closed it behind him, Aidan used his phone screen to look for Jack. Not seeing him, he headed for the area behind the wardrobe.

Jack was sitting on the floor, one leg drawn up with his arm resting on it. "Are you going to tell me what happened?"

It was the last thing he wanted to do. Although it wouldn't surprise him if Jack already thought he was an idiot. He sat on the floor. "You need furniture in here. Something to sit on. Come winter this floor is going to be freezing."

Jack shrugged. "I don't feel the heat or cold."

"What about the people you're meant to help? Do you think they'll want to hang out with you in here during winter?"

"Must have been pretty bad if this is all you can come up with to get out of talking about it."

He fell silent, staring at Jack for a moment. "Yeah." He dropped his head into his hands, covering his face, his words half muffled. "I'm an idiot."

"Aren't we all at times? You can't have done any worse than me."

He raised his head to look at Jack and had to turn his screen on again. That was right, Jack had mentioned shooting his girlfriend after she'd stabbed him. "Did she survive?" When Jack didn't answer straight away he started to clarify the question.

"No."

He wanted to ask Jack what had happened, but that word had sounded very much like 'quit bothering me'. He also should probably tell Jack what had happened at his father's place, rather than worry about events that had occurred decades ago. Before he had a chance to speak, his phone rang. He stared at the display. It read 'Private'.

Jack leaned forward to look at the screen. "You don't want to answer it?"

"I think it might be my dad. Or Phil."

"You don't want to talk to them?"

He shook his head. The phone stopped ringing and instantly started again.

"Looks like they want to talk to you. Or at least someone does."

"Yeah." He continued to watch the screen until it eventually rang out again. As before, it started to ring straight away.

"Looks like they're too thick to get the message you're not interested in talking."

He supposed he'd have to answer. Either that or turn his phone off. If he did turn it off and his grandmother tried to ring, she might be worried enough to come looking for him. He didn't want her anywhere near Phil.

Chapter Nine

Aiden

Aiden answered the call. "What?"

"Where are you?" Gary asked.

"Why did you ask me to move in with you?" He knew what he'd overheard, but he was still hoping there was another reason.

"Don't try and change the subject. Where are you? And you'd better have the parcel on you."

"If you tell me why, I'll tell you where the parcel is."

"There's no point now, Mum's ruined you."

The answer probably wasn't going to be one he liked, but he couldn't stop demanding the truth. He needed the words. "Why? That's all I want to know. Why?"

"I thought we could work together. Be a team,

like when you were a little kid. We were the perfect team."

Yep, it was official. He was a complete and utter idiot. He didn't remember a lot from those years, but he remembered regularly playing the part of a lost child to distract people for his father. Afterwards his father would buy him a bag of lollies and tell him how great he'd been. It had been years before he'd realised what had actually been going on. Obviously he'd always been an idiot.

"You still there, Aiden?"

"Yeah."

"Where's the parcel?"

He should have known that was all his father had wanted to ask. "With me."

"Where are you?"

He smiled at the anger and frustration he could hear in his father's voice. "With the parcel." He almost laughed at the growling sound his father made. A grim feeling of satisfaction settled over him.

"Phil isn't a man you want to annoy."

He was sick of this. He should have known better. What had made him think his father was any more interested in having him in his life than his mother had been? "That sounds like your problem, not mine."

"It's your problem. And if you don't get the parcel to Phil shortly, it'll be your grandmother's problem too. You've got fifteen minutes to think about it." Gary disconnected.

Aiden had no idea what to do. It was impossible to think clearly with how fast his heart raced and the words that rang out over and over again in his mind. 'Your grandmother's problem.'

"Do you want to tell me what happened when you went home?"

Not at all, but he guessed he should. Maybe Jack would know what to do. There was no way he wanted anything to happen to his grandmother. She annoyed him at times with how much she fussed over him, but he didn't doubt she wanted him in her life. She was obviously the only family who did.

He told Jack what had happened, continually checking the time. There were three minutes left of the fifteen his father had given him by the time he'd finished speaking.

"You need to tell your grandmother she's in danger."

"Dad wouldn't hurt his own mum."

"What about Phil?"

He felt sick at the idea, dialling his home number. His grandmother didn't have a mobile phone and had told him numerous times she was too old for one and the landline was more than adequate for her needs.

"What has you up at half past six? The last time you were up this early on Easter Sunday was because you still believed in the Easter bunny and wanted to catch a glimpse of him."

He couldn't resist smiling at her teasing tone. "Happy Easter, Grandma."

"Good thing you were up early. I've got to leave in half an hour. The girls talked me into helping at the local Easter fair. I have no idea what they expect me to do."

Relief washed over him. She was going out. Phil wouldn't have any way of finding her. "When will you be home?"

"Oh, not till late. I'll be lucky to be home before supper."

"Dinner." He automatically corrected her.

"You can have dinner, I'll have supper."

Some of his fear faded at the familiar words. She was okay. "Have fun, Grandma. Call me when you get home and you can tell me what they made you do."

"Are you okay?"

"Yeah."

"Are you sure? I'm pretty certain I heard you tell me I was allowed to ring you."

"Very funny." He kept his tone dry, not wanting to give anything else away. "I'll talk to you later." He'd be okay as soon as he figured out what to do. At least now he didn't have to worry about his grandmother for a bit. He'd tell her about Phil and Gary later. He dreaded to think how that conversation would go. She wouldn't be angry, but she'd get that sad look in her eyes. The one that talking about her son always brought.

When he hung up, he saw it was past the time for his father to ring. He smiled, feeling that same grim satisfaction again, glad he'd been on the phone when his father had probably tried to call. Wanting to annoy Gary even further, he rang Karina.

Her greeting was a sleepy mumble.

"What are you doing?" Jack demanded.

Aidan ignored Jack, speaking to Karina instead. "Can you say that again? I didn't understand a single word."

"You better have a good reason for ringing so early. It's not even seven."

"Happy Easter."

"Nope. Not good enough. Not unless it comes with lots of chocolate."

Aidan chuckled. "How about if I bring chocolate when I visit you?"

"Today?"

"Well…" his voice trailed off. He hadn't planned to see her today, but he had to do something while he thought about what he should do. Spending time with Karina always put him in a good mood. Maybe that would help him come up with some ideas.

"Please."

"What do you think you're doing?" Jack asked again. "Are you out of your tree?"

He nearly laughed, but managed to stop himself in time. Karina probably would have taken it the wrong way. How could he not be crazy? Not only was he talking to a ghost, who used a phrase he understood because he'd heard his grandmother use it, but he'd also believed every word his father had told him Friday night. "Why don't we meet in the city?"

"The problem won't go away by ignoring it," Jack warned. "Don't you care about what happens to your grandmother?"

He closed his eyes, focusing on his phone call. "Well? What do you say?"

"Why don't you come here for the day?" Karina asked.

"You're a blasted idiot."

Aidan opened his eyes in time to see Jack stride through the wardrobe. He really wished Jack wouldn't do that. "I've got things to do with my dad after lunch." That should give him enough time to figure out what to do. Hopefully. It would take half the amount of time to get back from the city than it would from Karina's place.

"Okay. I'll find out what time Mum can drop me in there and text you."

"Talk her into as soon as possible since I've got stuff to do after lunch."

"I'll see what I can do."

Chapter Ten

Aiden

Aiden was still smiling when he hung up. The smile disappeared when he looked at the back of the wardrobe Jack had disappeared through. What was he going to do with the jewellery? If he did as Jack suggested and took them to the police, how could he prove they were Phil's? He could easily say he knew nothing about them and they were trying to frame him.

He rose to his feet, yawning. Good thing he'd slept in yesterday morning. He needed to grab a coffee in the city. Or two. When he stepped out of the groundsman's shed, he saw Jack leaning against a tree, looking in his direction. His first thought was to defend himself. His second was that it was his life, not Jack's.

Jack pushed away from the tree. "Do you think you might lead them to whoever you're meeting?"

Aiden shook his head. "Impossible. How would they know where I'm going?" He looked from the tree to Jack. "I thought you said you can't touch anything. How can you lean against a tree?"

"I can't. It just looks like I am. It's habit. Are you sure they aren't watching you, waiting for a chance to get that parcel off you?"

"They're not the sort of people to sit back and watch. If they knew where I was, they'd have already done something about it. I wouldn't be meeting up with Karina if I thought she could get hurt." He wasn't about to tell Jack exactly how much Karina meant to him, but if he'd known, Jack wouldn't even have suggested that.

"Running away from the problem won't fix it. I can tell you that from experience."

"I'm not running away. I'm taking some time to think about what to do." His phone beeped and he saw it was a message from Karina giving him a location and time. "I've got to go. I need to be in the city by nine and I still have to find the closest bus stop." Luckily he had Internet access on his phone so it shouldn't take too long to find out.

"Why not go to the fuzz?"

"Because I can't prove Phil gave the jewellery to my dad. Otherwise I would." He thought about how many years he'd waited for his father to get out of jail. In all his numerous daydreams not once had the occasion been like this. He was almost embarrassed by how he'd expected their reunion to turn out. "I'll be back later." He started to walk towards the fence when his phone rang. Seeing it was a private number, he hesitated. He was tempted to turn his phone off. He answered it instead. "What?"

"Bring me the parcel and Phil said he'd forget this ever happened."

"Yeah, right." Phil hadn't looked like the sort to forgive and forget. It was obvious that even his father thought him an idiot.

"You're trying my patience."

He opened his mouth to argue, then wondered what was the point. He disconnected the call and turned his phone off. He continued to stare down at it, surprised by his actions.

"You're not going to freak out are you?"

Aiden turned to Jack, who'd come to stand beside him. "What?"

"You've got a strange expression on your face, like you're about to lose the plot."

"Oh." He couldn't think what to say, then

wondered why he should be worried about reassuring Jack. "I'll see you later." He continued walking to the fence, vaulting over it when he reached it. He wondered if it was safe to turn the phone on long enough to figure out where the closest bus stop was. In the end, he didn't need to. He headed for the steady noise of traffic he could hear and found a main road. A bus shelter was in sight and he strode towards it.

The trip into the city was uneventful and he dozed in his seat, nearly missing his stop. He reached where he was to meet Karina nearly half an hour early. Not enough time to grab a coffee and something to eat before she arrived. He'd missed dinner and it was way past breakfast time. He thought of the chocolate he'd promised to buy her and wondered if she'd accept a meal instead.

Karina's mother's car pulled up and Karina hopped out. She was nearly as tall as him with long legs and, as she put it, colourless hair that was perfect for dyeing. Today it was red and black, a few weeks ago it had been a blue that matched her eyes. He'd never seen her hair its natural blond colour. Waving goodbye to her mother she turned and spotted him, hurrying in his direction.

Aiden strode towards her, reaching her as her

mother's car disappeared amongst the traffic. He wrapped his arms around her, tighter than usual, and kissed her like they'd been separated for years instead of days.

When Karina eventually drew slightly away from him, she grinned. "Maybe you should go away more often."

He laughed, keeping his arms around her, glad he didn't have to explain the real reason why he'd clung to her so tightly. He didn't want to let her go, but knew he'd have to sooner or later. With how hungry he was, it was probably going to be sooner. He also needed a coffee to help keep him awake. "Have you had breakfast yet?"

"You didn't think I was going to last this long without eating, did you?"

He shrugged. "How about we find a cafe that sells something chocolatey?"

"That shouldn't be too hard. Not on Easter Sunday."

He dropped one arm, still keeping the other around her. Like Karina had said, it didn't take them long to find a cafe serving something with chocolate. He ordered breakfast and an extra strong coffee, while she had chocolate mousse topped by grated chocolate.

He eyed her food in its large, fancy bowl. "You're going to make yourself sick eating all of that."

Karina dipped her spoon back in the mousse. "It'll be worth it." She held out the spoon. "Want some?"

He couldn't resist her smile and the hint of challenge in her eyes. "I guess someone needs to help you so you don't make yourself sick on all that chocolate." The normalcy of the morning made the rest of his weekend seem impossible. Like something from a movie he'd watched. Why hadn't his father been interested in getting to know him? Why had he only wanted someone to run cons with him? He pushed the uncomfortable thoughts from his mind, unable to get rid of the one that kept intruding. Why didn't his father want him just because he was his son?

Numerous times when he'd been struggling with a problem, his grandmother had told him to set it aside and do something else. Give his brain a chance to think on the problem rather than pressuring it. He only hoped her advice worked this time. Providing he could stop dwelling on the problem.

The rest of the morning passed far too quickly. Karina dragged him into a shop where he bought her some bunny shaped chocolates and they stopped to listen to some buskers playing on the footpath. Karina convinced him to dance with her and half embarrassed, half amused, he did. They wandered through a couple of shops, ran into some friends, talked, laughed and kissed. When they sat down for lunch, Aiden lost his good mood. Karina's mum would be picking her up soon and he still had no idea what to do about the jewellery. He'd considered asking the mates he'd run into for some help, but didn't want to put anyone else at risk. It was bad enough he'd accidentally involved his grandmother in the problem.

"What's wrong?"

He shook his head, trying to smile.

"Don't give me that. I know you."

"I should hope so." He tried to keep his tone light and teasing. He guessed he must have been successful when she laughed.

"That's okay, I'll get you to tell me eventually." She changed her voice to a terrible imitation of a movie bad guy. "We have ways of making you talk."

He couldn't resist grinning, recapturing some of his earlier mood. "I don't want the day to end." He sobered. "I've been thinking I'll probably stay at my grandma's."

"You will? Is that because you miss me?"

What could he say? He wasn't a complete idiot. "That's one of the reasons. A really important reason."

Karina laughed, reaching across the table to take his hand. "Okay, I'd like to think that was true. What's the real reason?"

He knew she wouldn't laugh at him and would more than likely be sympathetic, but he couldn't bring himself to tell her what had happened. He shrugged. "There's a lot of things I'd miss about living at Grandma's. Maybe I'll see Dad on weekends." He doubted his grandmother would let him visit his father in prison. She never had before. "Besides, changing schools partway through year twelve is considered rather crazy."

Karina laughed. "I seem to recall someone very wise making that comment."

"Very wise, huh?"

"Yes. Wouldn't you agree?" She tilted her head at an angle, still smiling.

"Absolutely." He grinned. "I'm not crazy enough to disagree."

She laughed again. "You do know you're going to have to pay for that comment, don't you?"

He rose to his feet, still holding her hand. "I'm sure of it, but at least I'll be around to accept my punishment." He hoped. There was always the chance things could go very wrong. He wondered if many people became ghosts when they died. If he died these holidays would he become one? Jack had talked about atonement. He'd certainly done a lot of illegal things when he was a kid. Did it count if you didn't know any better?

Karina stood up and walked beside him to where she'd planned to meet her mother. "Are you okay? You've got that look again."

"I've still got to talk to my dad."

"Oh."

"Yeah, oh." He smiled wryly. If she'd known exactly what that conversation would be about she probably would have chosen a different word.

Chapter Eleven

Aiden

By the time Aiden and Karina reached where they were to meet Karina's mum, she was already there waiting. Aiden had barely pressed his lips to Karina's before her mum was hitting the horn.

Drawing away, Karina laughed. "At least it's not my dad. He would have got out of the car and come over to fetch me. I'll call you later."

He turned on his phone as he watched her disappear, expecting her to send him a text as usual. And there it was, the moment his phone finished turning on. *Miss you already.* He didn't reply, knowing she didn't expect one. He left his phone on, wondering if he should call his father or wait until he rang again. Sliding his phone back into his pocket, he decided to wait. He still had no idea what to do.

Somehow he needed to get this all sorted before his grandmother returned home for the evening. That didn't give him much time.

He had no idea what to do. Remembering how hungry he'd been when he'd arrived in the city and not knowing how long it'd take to sort everything out, he decided to buy snacks for later.

Spotting a convenience store, he headed in that direction. His luck obviously hadn't improved because there was a line up and before his turn, the customer in front dropped a glass bottle of sauce that needed to be cleaned up before anyone else was served. He was tempted to go elsewhere, but decided there was no guarantee he'd be served any quicker, not with the way his luck was lately. He pressed his lips together, trying not to say something. Looking away from the mess, he spotted a rack of newspapers.

He read the headlines. There was one he had to read twice to make sure he hadn't misread it. 'Jewellery Nest Egg Stolen. Elderly Couple Devastated.' Phil had stolen from an elderly couple? He picked up a copy of the paper. Maybe it was some other theft and not Phil's. Once he was back at the school he'd read it over and find out for certain.

Stepping up to the counter, he placed all the items down, grabbing a couple of Easter eggs from the display. He might need them when the coffee wore off. The girl behind the counter seemed to take forever and twice he nearly told her to hurry up. Finally she totalled up his bill and he paid her, biting back the impatient comment he was tempted to make.

Striding out of the convenience store, he slid his purchases into his backpack before heading towards the closest bus stop. Partway down the street, he saw a car pull up and his father get out. He froze. What was he doing here? Was it a coincidence? When he saw Gary look in his direction, he turned and headed back the way he'd come, hoping to lose himself in the crowded shopping complex he'd passed.

Reaching the entrance, he peered back into the street and saw his father was headed directly towards him. It was impossible. How had he found him? As he watched, his father glanced at the phone he held as he continued to stride forward. Swearing, Aiden reached for his phone and turned it off, running through the complex towards the street entrance at the other end. He remembered logging into an app on a tablet several months ago when he'd misplaced his phone and how easy it had been to find it. So much for thinking his father wouldn't be able to find him. Jack had been right. Again. Although he had no idea how his father had been able to use that app since he'd had to put in a password. He thought of Phil. If the man could steal a fortune in jewellery, hacking a password would probably be easy. Or at least easy to find someone willing to do it for him.

The crowd thinned before he reached the other end of the complex. Fearing his father might see him, he ducked into a shop and hid behind a mannequin. He held his breath and watched as his father slowly walked past, looking in every direction. He remained behind the mannequin, wanting to make sure his father was well and truly out of sight before he left the shop. He slowly let out his breath as his father moved out of view.

Someone tapped him on the shoulder and breathing in sharply, he spun, ready to run. A shop assistant stood in front of him, wearing a name badge with Phil written on it. Aiden nearly laughed at the irony of it. This Phil was shorter than him, had a receding hairline and wore glasses.

"Can I help you?" The tone clearly said he doubted it.

"Uhm, sorry." Telling this man he was hiding from his father would probably get him kicked out of the store. "I was trying to avoid being seen by an ex."

"Ahh." Phil nodded, his expression becoming

sympathetic. "Say no more, I perfectly understand." He went from nodding to slowly shaking his head, releasing a heavy sigh. "The stories I could tell." Another long sigh. "Take as much time as you need."

"Thanks." He watched as Phil wandered off to pester another customer before peering around the mannequin again. He couldn't see his father anywhere. He had no idea what to do. He couldn't stay here the rest of the afternoon. He had to pick a direction to take. Did he go in the direction he'd last seen his father heading or in the opposite one? If only the sales assistant hadn't distracted him he'd know where his father had gone. It took a few minutes to decide to go in the opposite direction, back the way he'd come.

He kept looking over his shoulder and into each shop he passed. He didn't see one single person he knew. He'd almost reached the street when he saw his father come out of a shop ahead of him. He froze for a moment before turning and running back to the last shop, ducking inside. He'd obviously chosen the wrong direction. Looking around he saw that not only had he chosen the wrong direction, but he'd chosen the wrong shop. Ladies lingerie wasn't the best place to hide.

Feeling his face heat, he turned towards the

entrance and looked for his father. He was relieved to see him step out onto the street and turn a corner, disappearing from view. A glance behind him showed a smiling shop assistant coming his way. He hurriedly left the store before she could reach him, turning in the opposite direction he'd seen his father take. This time he reached the other street entrance without incident, but he didn't relax. There was still a chance his father would find him and he didn't know where Phil was. For all he knew, he could be in the area too. It had been a stupid idea heading into the city. It hadn't helped him at all.

He zigzagged through streets, a couple of shopping centres and eventually headed for a bus stop. Hopefully his father had lost track of him and it'd be safe to return to the school. The entire trip back, he kept looking out the windows, half expecting to see Gary or Phil. Every stop the bus made to collect another passenger had him holding his breath and staring at the doorway as he waited to see if either of them would enter.

He made it back to the main road, not far from the school, without seeing either of them. It took a lot of effort to step out of the bus and into the open when it reached his stop. He felt on edge and didn't know if it was from too much coffee or constantly looking over his shoulder. A glance around showed he was still safe, but he felt exposed on the main street. He ran most of the way back to the school, wanting to get out of sight.

Chapter Twelve

Aiden

Reaching the fence, Aiden vaulted over it and strode towards the groundsman's shed. The door was still unlocked, but Jack wasn't inside. The jewellery was. He'd just finished checking on it and was about to start looking for Jack when the ghost strode through the wardrobe.

"I really wish you wouldn't do that." It was unnerving seeing someone walk through something solid.

"Do what?"

"Walk through things."

"You want me to go around it when I can easily walk through it?"

Aiden shrugged, then nodded. It sounded

ridiculous when it was put like that. "Never mind." He had more important things to worry about.

"What's your hang-up?"

"What?"

"You're acting like you're about to lose your cool. So what's the problem?"

He slowly shook his head. Jack was a little hard to understand sometimes. "You were kind of right." Jack must think he was clueless.

"About what?"

"They can find me, but only when I have my phone turned on." He told Jack everything that had happened while he'd been gone. Well, not quite everything. He glossed over the time he'd spent with Karina. Remembering the newspaper he'd bought, he took it out of his backpack and turned to the page with the article he wanted to read. He scanned the words, his heart sinking with each one. He obviously didn't know his father at all. And he was beginning to think he didn't want to know him.

"Hold the paper so I can read it." Jack moved closer to him.

"There's nothing good in the article." He turned the paper so Jack could read it too. "The jewellery was basically their retirement fund. I have no idea why they didn't put their money in the bank. It would have been more secure than jewellery in a safe. Obviously." He'd already known Phil wasn't a nice person, but there'd still been a small hope that his father was. How could he be if he was hanging out with someone like Phil? He stared at the image of the elderly couple in the paper. The woman reminded him a little of his own grandmother. Her and her husband looked devastated.

"What are you going to do?"

"I don't know, but whatever it is I need to do it before Grandma gets home." There was no way he was going to let anything happen to her. Phil obviously didn't care who he hurt. Even elderly people were fair game to him.

"How long do we have to come up with a plan?"

He didn't have a clue and he wasn't about to turn on his phone to check. "I'm not sure. We need to be finished before dark." His gaze was drawn back to the newspaper images of the jewellery. The photos were a little grainy, but he recognised them from the parcel. Somehow he had to get them back to their owners. They didn't deserve to have them stolen. According to the paper, they'd already suffered more than enough hardships in their lives.

"We've got three or four hours before dark." Jack

sat in the spot he'd been in earlier, drawing one leg up. "What do you want to see happen?"

It felt odd to stand while Jack was sitting. He joined him on the floor. "Phil in jail and the jewellery with the proper owners." He started to say his father not in jail, but he couldn't bring himself to speak the words. He'd been so wrong about Gary. No wonder his grandmother tried to avoid speaking about him. She hated being negative about people. But it looked like there wasn't any other way to be when talking about Gary. Or thinking about him.

"What else?"

Aiden shrugged. "No one to get hurt."

Jack laughed mockingly. "Then you're probably asking the wrong person for help."

"I didn't ask for help, you offered."

"No, I was volunteered. There's a difference."

"Not much of one. You let yourself be volunteered." He paused. "Have you got any ideas?"

"Not yet. At least we have a way of getting them here once we come up with a plan."

Aiden frowned. "What do you mean?"

"Turn on your phone and they can track you again."

"Oh." He mentally berated himself for not thinking of that earlier. "All right. That's one part sorted. Next we have to figure out how to get the cops here." He remembered how his grandmother had got a fright last year thinking someone was breaking in, but it had been a possum. She'd already called 000 before he'd checked to see what was going on and they'd learned it was nothing to worry about. She'd hung up before emergency had answered and they'd called her back.

He'd laughed at how embarrassed she'd been trying to explain what had happened. She'd chased him off to bed and told him not to mock his elders. He smiled as he thought about the moment.

"Did you think of something?"

"Possibly." He told Jack about the possum episode. "I'll wait for Dad and Phil to arrive before I ring 000 and leave the call connected. If I put the phone somewhere they can't reach it, then they can't turn it off. They'll be busy tracking down my phone while I'll be hiding somewhere until the police get here."

"What if they find you before the police arrive?"

Aiden shrugged. "The plan's not perfect, but it's the best I can come up with." Maybe he'd get lucky for a change.

"We'll see if we can find somewhere to hide the phone that's not in view of the perimeter of the school before we turn it on. That way I can watch for them and warn you before they have a chance to find you."

"Okay." That sounded like a good plan. He rose to his feet. "Let's do this." Before he changed his mind. He was already having second thoughts.

Chapter Thirteen

Aiden

It took longer than Aiden had thought to find somewhere suitable to hide the phone. Jack also unlocked a nearby classroom for him to hide in and gave him a tour of the school grounds, unlocking several more classrooms in case he wasn't able to hide in time and needed to make a run for it. He hoped it didn't come to that. The plan hinged on them being there when the police arrived and somehow convincing the police that Phil was after him because he'd hidden the jewellery Phil had stolen. After the tour, they returned to where Aiden planned to hide the phone.

It was a stormwater drain that was currently dry. The grate was padlocked into place and it was too narrow to get a hand through, but he'd be able to drop his phone in there. Another thought occurred to him.

"What about alarms?" He didn't need some security company turning up and getting in the way.

"What alarms?"

"Don't the classroom doors have them?"

Jack chuckled, nodding his head. "I've lost count of the number of times the alarm system has been changed or checked because doors have been unlocked or opened during the night. What I do to unlock the door also prevents the alarm from working. You don't have to worry about any of them going off."

"That's good." He stared at the phone he held.

"Are you going to turn it on?"

He should, but for some reason he couldn't bring himself to press the button. "Have we forgotten anything?" He couldn't stop thinking about Phil. The man was taller and broader than him and looked like he knew how to fight. He'd only ever been in a few schoolyard fights. Nothing major. What if Phil got a hold of him?

"Not that I can think of." Jack stared at him for a moment. "You don't have to do this. Go home to your grandmother and the two of you can go to the police."

He shook his head. He wasn't about to drag his grandmother any further into his mess. He was the one who'd been stupid enough to believe Gary so he should be the one to sort it out. "I was going over everything and making sure we hadn't forgotten anything." That sounded far better than he was terrified to turn on the phone. He forced himself to push the button and watched as the screen lit up. Once everything had loaded, there were a couple of messages. Checking, he found they were from his father. Each sounded more impatient than the last with the final one telling him to get home if he knew what was good for him.

He did know what was good for him and it wasn't going back to his father's place. He met Jack's gaze. "It's on."

Jack nodded. "I'll keep an eye out for them."

"Wait." He flicked through the photos on his phone and brought up one of his father. "I don't have one of Phil, but this is my dad."

Jack stared at the picture for a few seconds before nodding and striding towards the front of the school.

Aiden watched him walk through all the objects. It didn't seem as disconcerting this time. It meant Jack would reach him well before Gary and Phil, as they'd have to go around everything. He checked the time on his phone. It was nearly four o'clock. It was hard to believe it was so late. Everything had taken much longer than he'd planned. He looked in the direction Jack had taken. Would he recognise them in plenty of time to let him know? He had to ring emergency, drop the phone into the storm drain and hide himself. What if they came from a different direction? Just because that was the direction his father lived in, it didn't mean he'd come from there. He checked the time again. Only five minutes had passed.

He felt like pacing, but managed to stay still. Where were they? Had they given up looking for him? Were they going to wait for his grandmother to return home instead? Maybe he should ring and tell his father where to meet him. But why would his father come here? And would he expect a trap? What had made him think this plan would even work? He looked at the time. Only another four minutes had passed.

He was going to go crazy waiting. He fought the urge to pace. Actually, it was probably more like an urge to run. Reminding himself they'd threatened his grandmother was all that kept him from running. How much longer would they be? He was about to check the time again when he heard Jack shout.

"They're coming."

Aiden nearly dropped the phone. He also had to try twice to dial 000. It wasn't like it was a difficult number. You couldn't get more simple than three zeros. He started to drop it in the storm drain, but stopped. What if it turned off when it landed?

Jack reached his side. "Hurry."

He put the phone to his ear and listened to it ringing.

"What are you doing?" Jack looked behind him.

The operator answered and he quickly spoke. "Help. They want to kill me." He rattled off the address of the school. The operator was asking him questions when he dropped the phone in the drain and ran for the classroom, slipping through the door that he closed softly behind himself. He crouched beneath a window, pressing his back to the wall, his breath harsh in the silence. He forced himself to breathe slower, trying not to panic. It was too late now to change his mind.

Jack stood beside him, looking out the window. "I thought we agreed you were going to drop it and run."

"I wanted to make sure they knew it wasn't a prank and they knew where to find me if the phone turned off when it landed in the drain." He kept his voice as low as possible. "Can you see them?"

"They've reached the drain and are staring down at it. Your father is crouching beside it and trying to get it open. Now he's shaking his head."

He wanted to check out the window himself, but that probably wasn't a good idea. He certainly didn't want to risk being seen. "What's happening now?"

"Be quiet and I'll tell you if anything changes. Phil has pulled out a gun and is holding it to the grate. I think he's going to shoot your phone."

For one crazy moment, Aiden started to rise. He held himself still. It was only a phone. There wasn't much on it he couldn't replace. He'd backed it up only a couple of weeks ago so he wouldn't even lose many photos. When the noise came, he flinched.

"He shot your phone. I'll be back in a minute."

He wanted to protest, but Jack had walked through the wall before he had a chance. When Jack returned, he glared up at him. It was annoying not being able to talk and demand what was going on.

"Your phone is dead. Let's hope the people you called will still turn up."

He hoped so too. Actually, he hoped they were already on the way.

"They've spread out and started to search for you."

"Aiden!"

He shuddered at the anger in his father's voice. Had

he ever really known the man? A few short visits in the past six months obviously hadn't been enough to show him what Gary was like. It made him wonder about his mother. Maybe he was lucky she wasn't in his life.

"They're moving out of sight and seem to be checking the area together now. I'll follow them and see what they're up to." Jack walked through the wall again.

Aiden took a deep breath, trying to ignore his father who called his name three more times. He hoped they didn't give up looking for him. They had to stay nearby if the plan was to work. Not that it was much of a plan. He was beginning to realise he'd left far too much to chance.

Jack walked through the wall opposite him. "Get over this side. They're coming around to the back of the building."

Chapter Fourteen

Aiden

Remaining in a crouch, Aiden hurried across the room, slowed down by the desks and chairs in his way. He'd nearly reached the wall when Phil looked through the window. He froze.

Phil raised his gun. "Get out here or I'll shoot."

Gary joined him. "Don't shoot him. We'll never find the parcel if you do that."

The momentary relief he'd felt at his father's initial words, faded. He couldn't believe Gary thought a handful of jewellery were more important than his own son. Pain arrowed through him from his father's words.

"What are you waiting for?" Jack demanded. "Run." He ran for the door and it flew open as he rushed through it.

Aiden ran after him, leaving the door open behind him. He heard the sound of a gun firing and flinched. He wasn't about to stick around to see what had been shot. Heading for the next hiding place, he forced himself not to look behind. It would only slow him down.

Jack stood by the stairs that were on the other side of a building. He watched behind Aiden. "Quick. They're still not in sight."

Aiden raced up the stairs, trying to be as quiet as possible. He slipped inside the unlocked classroom and couldn't resist looking out the window on the far side of the room.

Jack strode through a wall. "What do you think you're doing? Don't be a ditz. Get your head down before they see you."

"Where are they?" He sat on the floor.

"Near this building."

"What if they come up here? I'll be trapped."

"I'll lead them away. I'll open the doors of some of the other classrooms."

He opened his mouth to agree, but Jack had already left. A minute later he heard the slamming of classroom doors. Then a couple of minutes later several more doors slammed open in the opposite direction. He couldn't resist checking out the windows. He couldn't see Gary or Phil in either direction. That didn't make him feel any better. He worried they might have left the area.

"Get out here now." Phil's voice rang out over the school grounds.

Aiden's relief at hearing he was still in the area was short lived when Phil continued to talk.

"You have five minutes to get out here or I'm ringing someone to go collect your grandma."

Aiden rose to his feet. He had no choice. He slowly walked towards the door. The police mustn't be coming. They'd probably thought it was a prank. He'd believed his grandmother was safe, but she wouldn't be if there was someone waiting for her when she got home. He hadn't thought of that. There was no way to warn her even if his phone hadn't been shot. He reached for the door, jumping back when Jack stepped through it. His heart raced. "You've got to stop doing that." Jack gave him a look that Aiden clearly recognised as someone mentally calling him an idiot. He couldn't argue with that. Not when he clearly was. Look at the mess he'd made of his life over the past few days. Starting with believing his father Friday night.

"What do you think you're doing?"

"I thought that was obvious. Get out of my way."

"What's wrong with kids these days? Haven't any of you got a sense of self preservation?"

Aiden laughed, a short sharp sound that was unfamiliar to him. "I guess nothing's changed then. Otherwise you wouldn't have died at eighteen. Get out of my way, Jack. I'm not about to let them hurt my grandma."

Jack stood in the way a few more seconds before he stepped aside. "I have to start coming up with better plans."

Aiden strode out of the classroom and down the stairs. Jack remained beside him. He saw Phil and Gary before they spotted him. When Phil turned in his direction, he pointed the gun at him. Aiden stopped abruptly, his eyes drawn to the weapon Phil held. His heart raced and it was all he could do not to turn and run.

"Keep moving. I can still make that call."

Aiden forced himself to walk forwards, each step an effort. What if Phil shot him after all? He managed to drag his gaze away from the gun long enough to glance at his father. There'd be no help there. He looked as angry as Phil.

"I haven't got all day," Phil growled.

Aiden stopped when he was several metres from Phil. He came up with and discarded numerous plans, each more ridiculous than the last. There was no way of escaping. If he tried to run, Phil would probably shoot him. He glanced towards Jack. Even though he was a ghost and no one else could see him, he still felt better having him at his side. He didn't know if he could have managed to face Phil alone.

"Where's my parcel?" Phil continued to point the gun at Aiden.

"Once he has it, he's got no reason to keep you alive," Jack said.

He glanced towards Jack. He hadn't needed the ghost to tell him that. He'd already figured it out on his own.

"It's that way?" Phil pointed the gun in the direction Aiden had glanced.

Aiden shook his head. "If I get the parcel for you, will you leave my grandma and me alone?"

"There's nothing to stop him from breaking his word to you," Jack said.

At the same time as Jack spoke, Phil laughed. "You've got to be kidding. Do you really think I'm going to let you get away with everything you've done? I'll leave the old woman alone, kid." He pointed at him with the gun, the weapon momentarily coming a little closer as if it was used for emphasis. "But you need to be taught a lesson. I'll be giving you that hiding your father should have given you." Phil laughed again. "And what better place to learn a lesson than at a school? Just think of me as your teacher and call me sir."

When Gary sniggered, Aiden glared at him. He guessed he was going to have to accept those terms. No one was coming to his rescue. The plan had been a failure. "All right."

"Lead the way," Phil said.

Aiden did, almost feeling the gun pointed at his back. It took all his willpower not to run. His movements felt jerky and forced.

"No self preservation," Jack muttered.

Aidan opened his mouth to argue, but closed it again, reminding himself only he could hear Jack. He continued to lead the way through the school grounds, ignoring Jack's frequent muttered comments and Phil's warning he better not be leading them the wrong way. Reaching the groundsman's shed Aiden stepped inside, leaving the door open. Jack followed him into the dim interior and the door slammed shut behind him.

The door handle rattled. "Unlock this door now."

Aiden tried to step around Jack to let Phil inside.

Jack wouldn't let him. "They're not welcome in my place. Get the parcel and take it out to them."

Chapter Fifteen

Aiden

Aiden stared at Jack. It didn't take him long to decided the ghost wouldn't be budged. Ignoring Phil's threats, he hurried through the clutter and squeezed past the wardrobe. It took him nearly a minute to drag the parcel out from under it and he rushed back to the door. Jack stepped through and the door flew open.

Phil landed on the ground, swearing. Gary helped him up and Aiden stepped away from the door in case Jack decided to slam it shut again. Phil dusted himself off and Aiden stared at him, realising he'd dropped the gun. He spotted it at the same time as Phil did. He didn't have a chance to get past Phil and pick it up, but that didn't stop him from automatically leaning slightly in that direction.

Phil collected the gun and turned to him with a smile. "Something else you're going to pay for."

Aiden doubted that. Phil hadn't planned to go easy on him to start with. Nothing would change that.

"Hand over that parcel. Now." Phil pointed the gun at him again.

He swallowed hard, trying to make himself step forward.

"Police. Drop your weapons." The order came from the side of the groundsman's shed.

Relief made Aiden nearly collapse in a heap. He held himself in place. Phil continued to hold the gun on him. He also didn't have any idea how many police had arrived since the groundsman's shed was in the way. What if it was only two officers? Two against two made the odds far too even.

Phil stepped behind a tree, Gary running behind another one. The gun remained pointed towards Aiden.

"Throw out your weapons and come out with your hands where we can see them."

Phil peered around the edge of the tree, the gun still trained on Aiden. "This is all your fault."

Aiden heard the gunshot at the same time as Jack tackled him. He flew forwards, the parcel tumbling through the air to scatter jewellery across the ground.

He landed face first in the dirt and missed seeing Phil and Gary being captured while he lay there winded. He lifted his head in time to see them led away in handcuffs. Near him, on the ground, Jack was fading away. He reached for him.

"Guess the plan wasn't too bad after all." Jack grinned before he disappeared from sight.

A hand was held out and a pair of legs stood where Jack had been. "Do you need a hand up, son?"

Dazed, he took the hand and let the officer pull him to his feet. "Thanks." Looking around, he saw several officers collecting the scattered jewellery. He couldn't believe he was alive. Relief rushed through him, making him feel shaky.

"You're unharmed?" The officer eyed him up and down.

He nodded. Probably a little bruised, definitely shaken, but he was alive.

"Is there someone we can call to come to the station with you while you answer some questions?"

He shook his head and then nodded. "My grandma, but I don't know if she's home." He looked in the direction he'd left his phone. "I can't even call her. Phil shot my phone." He'd nearly ended up in the same condition as the phone.

"It's okay, son. We'll see if we can get hold of her for you."

He started to follow the officer, then remembered his backpack. He gestured towards the shed. "I hid my bag in there. I won't be a minute." When the officer nodded, he went inside and squeezed past the wardrobe. The picture of Rose caught his attention. He wanted to thank Jack, but had no idea how. The ghost had saved his life. He was still feeling more than a little dazed and shaken by that fact.

Grabbing his backpack, he started to turn towards the wardrobe. Instead his gaze was drawn to the floor where he'd sat with Jack. He smiled, lifting his gaze, hoping Jack could hear him. "I'll be back another day." He squeezed past the wardrobe and wound his way through the clutter to the officer who waited for him in the doorway.

Stepping outside, he pulled the door closed behind him. He was about to follow the officer, who had already started to walk away, when he heard the sound of the door locking. It was like hearing a friend say goodbye and it made him feel a little less shaky. "See you, Jack," he said under his breath before he strode after the officer.

Chapter Sixteen

Jack

Jack wandered through the empty school grounds, walking past one of the original buildings. They were all still here, the same buildings from when he'd attended school here in 1963. These days the newer buildings outnumbered them, but if he closed his eyes he could clearly see the way the place had once been. The silence pressed in on him and his steps slowed. Atonement was going to take far too long. The short spaces of time when he was able to talk to someone made the silences more difficult to endure.

He frowned, certain he heard his name called. Looking around, he heard it again, recognising the voice. It was Aiden. Striding in the direction of his place, he saw Aiden standing in front of the groundsman's shed. He clutched a brown cushion under one arm and kept glancing around the area. Jack had stopped expecting him to come back. It had been a week since he'd last seen him.

"Can you hear me, Jack? Where are you? It'd be helpful if you could open the door for me." Aiden glanced around again. "Come on, Jack. I did tell you I'd be back. Open the door."

Grinning, Jack strode forward. The door opened first try and he chuckled at Aiden's muttered comment.

"About time." Aiden wound his way through the clutter and squeezed past the wardrobe. He held out the cushion. "I have no idea where you are, so if I'm actually looking at a blank wall instead of you it's your own fault for not standing in the right place."

Jack chuckled again, already standing in front of Aiden. It had seemed the most logical place to be.

"I brought this for you. Well, for your visitors." He placed it on the floor, straightening up to look around. "I wish I could still see you. It seems strange talking to myself, but well…" he shrugged. "I wanted to let you know how everything went."

"It's good to see you. Thanks for the cushion." He knew Aiden couldn't hear him, but felt the need to say the words anyway. After a week of silence, the place felt like a graveyard. He always hated the school holidays and the Christmas ones were the worst. As hard as it was to be surrounded by people who couldn't see or hear him, being left alone with his own thoughts for weeks on end was more difficult.

Aiden cleared his throat. "You know this is a lot harder than I thought it would be. You saved my life. If you hadn't pushed me out of the way, I'd be dead." Aiden remained silent for a moment. "It's impossible to repay anyone for something like that. Even harder when it's a ghost you're trying to repay." Aiden gestured towards the cushion. "That isn't anywhere near what I owe you for everything you did. It'd be impossible to find anything that could do that." He cleared his throat again. "I hope you're a lot closer to getting that atonement you were talking about. Surely what you did for me will cancel out a heap of sins."

Jack hoped Aiden was right. "It'd be nice, but I doubt that blasted bird will see it the same way."

"Anyway, I wanted to tell you what's been happening the past week. Dad and Phil are in jail and likely to spend a very long time in there. I wanted to visit you sooner, but it's been crazy. Karina hassled me about not telling her what was going on. She said she knew me too well to not know something was wrong. Then she told me I could find out what it was like when she didn't tell me anything and she refused to answer my texts or phone calls. When she heard from one of my mates that I'd nearly been shot she called me, angry I hadn't told her and worried I'd nearly died. I hope you don't mind, I told everyone I tripped. I think if I had told them about you they would have been even more concerned for me."

Jack chuckled. "You've got that right. Look how much effort it took to convince you I'm a ghost."

"Grandma talked to me for hours about not lying to her. Even to protect her. She said that wasn't my job. I asked her if not protecting her included possums and she burst into tears. That wasn't the reaction I'd been aiming for. Anyway, when she stopped crying we finally had a good talk about my parents and I asked her if she knew where my mother was. I decided I should at least try and meet her. She said she'd talk to Dad and see if he knew where she was." Aiden's hands curled into fists and his expression hardened.

Jack wished Aiden could still see and hear him. "Blasted bird. What could a few more hours hurt?" Anger rush through him and he punched out at the back of the wardrobe, hating how little control he had over his existence. The wardrobe rocked slightly.

"Whoa." Aiden stepped away from the wardrobe,

eyeing it. "That's pretty much how I feel about him too. Especially after Grandma told me about her visit. Apparently my mum sent him a letter when I was three-years-old, wanting to see me. He didn't bother replying, just moved house so she couldn't get in touch with us again. He said the letter was in a box of old paperwork, Grandma was storing with the rest of his things, in her shed. It took her hours to find it, but when she did she visited the address on the letter. It is her parents' place and they were able to tell Grandma where she's living now." Aiden fell silent.

Jack wondered if he was going to have to try and get the wardrobe to rock again so Aiden would finish telling him everything.

"I talked to her two days ago. Apparently I've got two sisters. One is three years younger than me and the other is four years younger than me. They live in Sydney and my mum is flying up to meet me next week. She wants me to come stay with them for the next school holidays." Aiden smiled wryly. "I'm not sure I should go. Look how this school holiday, with a parent, turned out."

Jack chuckled. "Yeah, you might want to rethink that."

Aiden sighed. "I wish I could still see you. Or even hear you." He grinned. "Do you do Ouija boards?"

He sobered again. "Anyway, I'll come back and let you know how the visit goes. She sounds nice. Apart from all the tears when she realised who it was. Seriously. That's not the way to make a guy feel comfortable. I nearly hung up on her. I'll take Karina's anger over tears, any day." Aiden paused again. "The old couple got all their jewellery back. They wanted to see me and were so grateful it was awkward. But they did give me a reward. Enough that I'll be able to buy a car."

When Aiden remained silent for a long drawn out moment, Jack began to think he was finished. There were questions he wished he could have asked him and once again frustration and anger at the situation arrowed through him.

"I looked it up, you know. About what happened here. About killing your girlfriend and her new boyfriend. I didn't believe it at first, even though you kind of told me. I mean, you saved my life. It's hard to believe you also took lives. I couldn't stop thinking about it. Then after I talked to my mum and heard about everything that she was going through when she had me, I realised something. People like my dad, I don't think they can change. It's been ten years and he's exactly the same person he was when I last saw him. I didn't want to see that. I wanted him to be someone else. Someone better than he is. But I don't think he can be. And that's got nothing to do with me."

Jack nearly took a step back as Aidan's gaze stared directly towards him. It felt like Aiden knew exactly where he was.

"But other people, they can change. Like my mum. She's not the same person she was seventeen years ago. I don't know if that's better or not, but she has changed. She has a family and a life she sounds happy with. Her actions have created that life. Like your mum said, actions do speak louder than words."

Jack found himself nodding. His mother's actions had always spoken far louder than her words.

"And you Jack, I think you've changed too. I don't think you're the same person who took those lives."

He wanted to believe Aiden, but most of the time he still felt a lot like he'd always felt. Confused and no idea what he should be doing. And they said the teenage years were over far too quickly. Not for everyone they weren't.

"Anyway, I hope I haven't bored you too much." Aiden smiled wryly. "I'll understand if you leave your door locked next time I come knocking. But I really do hope you'll let me in."

Jack watched Aiden cross the small space between

him and the wardrobe. Aiden looked back towards him and Jack again felt like Aiden knew exactly where he was. "You can come back any time, Aiden."

"See you, Jack. Thanks for saving my life, mate." He squeezed between the wardrobe and the wall.

Jack walked through the wardrobe and followed Aiden outside. Aiden paused halfway to the fence and turned towards the shed with a grin and a wave, before striding to the fence and vaulting over it.

Jack stopped at the fence and watched Aiden disappear down the street. Silence descended, but this time it didn't seem to press in on him. School would be starting again soon. He probably should make the most of the quiet while he had the chance. With one last look up the street, he turned and headed back towards the groundsman's shed.

Free Ebook

Subscribe to Avril's newsletter to receive a free ebook. This ebook is exclusive to those on her mailing list. To find out more about this offer visit: http://www.avrilsabine.com/free-ebook/

*

We value your privacy and will not sell, rent, exchange or loan your email address to third parties. Your information is confidential and you are under no obligation to remain on the mailing list and can unsubscribe at any time.

Acknowledgements

Thanks to everyone who helped, particularly my editor for once again making sure this book was the best it could be. Thank you for being so demanding. I appreciate it.

To The Reader

If you enjoyed this book, why not consider leaving a review to help other readers discover it too? Reader engagement is one of the few ways that lets an author know readers want more books in a particular series or genre. So leave a review and tell friends, not only about this book but also about other ones you've enjoyed, so you can continue to enjoy books by your favourite authors for years to come.

Dreams are meant to be lived,

Avril.

About The Author

Avril is an Australian author who lives with her family on acreage in South East Queensland. She writes mostly young adult speculative fiction, but has been known to dabble in other genres. You can find more information about her at her website www.avrilsabine.com where you can also subscribe to her newsletter to be kept informed about new releases, current projects, blog posts and exclusive news.

Titles By Avril Sabine

Stories about strong characters and characters who discover their strengths.

SERIES

Assassins Of The Dead- Young Adult Fantasy/ Paranormal

Book 1: Dark Blade

Book 2: Dragon Touched

Book 3: Society Against Vampires

Book 4: King's Request

Dragon Blood- Young Adult Urban Fantasy (with elements of romance)

(5 book series)

Book 1: Pliethin

Book 2: Wyvern

Book 3: Surety

Book 4: Knight

Book 5: Mage

Dragon Mage- Young Adult Urban Fantasy (with elements of romance)

(Series two of Dragon Blood series)

Book 1: Promise

Dragon Blood Chronicles- Young Adult Urban Fantasy (with elements of romance)

(Companion stand alone series to Dragon Blood)

Book 1: Oath

Book 2: Betrayed

Guardians Of The Round Table- Young Adult Fantasy LitRPG

(Co-written with Storm and Rhys Petersen)

Book 1: Dexterity Fail

Book 2: Goblin Boots

Book 3: Singed Feathers

Book 4: Frog Mage

Book 5: Crystal Mine

Book 6: Cursed Harp

Rosie's Rangers- Young Adult Western Steampunk

(6 book series)

Book 1: Justice

Book 2: Vengeance

Book 3: Treachery

Book 4: Accused

Book 5: Wanted

Book 6: Corruption

Mark Of Kings- Children's Fantasy

(Upper middle grade/preteen)

(4 book series)

Book 1: The Arena

Book 2: The Island

Book 3: The Assassin

Book 4: The King

STAND ALONE SERIES

***Demon Hunters- Young Adult Urban Fantasy/
Horror (with elements of romance)***

Book 1: Blood Sacrifice

Book 2: Retribution

Book 3: Tainted

Book 4: Premonition

Book 5: Cursed

Book 6: Feud

Book 7: Extrication

Plea Of The Damned- Young Adult Urban Fantasy/Paranormal

(6 book series)

Book 1: Forgive Me Lucy

Book 2: Forgive Me Aiden

Book 3: Forgive Me Jena

Book 4: Forgive Me Kobe

Book 5: Forgive Me Marti

Book 6: Forgive Me Dawson

Realms Of The Fae- Young Adult Urban Fantasy (with elements of romance)

The Sword (short story in Like A Girl Anthology)

Heart Of Stone

Book 1: A Debt Owed

Book 2: Marked By The Hunt

Book 3: The Magic Collector

Book 4: An Unexpected Betrayal

Book 5: Imprisoned By Iron

Fairytales Retold (Short Stories)

Snow-White And Rose-Red

The Twelve Brothers

The Light Princess

Beauty And The Beast

Sleeping Beauty

Aschenputtel

The Golden Bird

The Frog Prince

The Death Of Koshchei The Deathless

Myths And Legends Retold (Short Stories)

Ion, Son Of Apollo

Sir Gawain And The Maid With The Narrow Sleeves

Princess Ilse, The Giant's Daughter

YOUNG ADULT NOVELS

Young Adult Fantasy (with elements of romance)

Elf Sight

Earth Bound

Young Adult Urban Fantasy

Stone Warrior (with elements of romance)

The Jungle Inside

Young Adult Contemporary (with elements of romance)

Through Your Eyes

The Ugly Stepsister

Perfect Little Princess

Young Adult Contemporary/Paranormal

Whispers In The Dark (with elements of romance and same sex relationships)

Over Too Soon (with elements of romance)

Young Adult Sci-Fi

Experiment X-One-Six (Urban Sci-Fi/Superheroes)

An Endless Dawn (Post Apocalyptic Sci-Fi)

CHILDREN'S BOOKS

Dragon Lord (Preteen/early teens) (Fantasy)

The Irish Wizard (Upper middle grade) (Urban Fantasy)

SHORT STORIES

Urban Fantasy

Eternally Late

Dealings With Joe

Glimpses (short story in That Moment When Anthology)

Contemporary

The Brat Next Door

Fantasy LitRPG

(Set in the same world as Guardians Of The Round Table Series)

Tales Of Inadon 1: The Disc (Co-written with Storm and Rhys Petersen) (short story in Game On! Anthology)

Post Apocalyptic Sci-Fi

Compulsive Directive

NONFICTION

A Year Of Weekly Writing Exercises (Creative Writing)

Cooking For Families With Allergies (Cooking) (Co-written with Storm Petersen)

Tell Me A Story, Grandma (Memoir)

For the most up to date details on available titles visit:

www.avrilsabine.com/books/bibliography

Plea Of The Damned Series

To learn more about this series visit:

www.avrilsabine.com/series/potd

BOOKS AVAILABLE IN THE PLEA OF THE DAMNED SERIES:

Book 1: Forgive Me Lucy

Book 2: Forgive Me Aiden

Book 3: Forgive Me Jena

Book 4: Forgive Me Kobe

Book 5: Forgive Me Marti

Book 6: Forgive Me Dawson

Disclaimer

This is a work of fiction. Names, characters, businesses, places, events and incidents are either the products of the author's imagination or used in a fictitious manner. Any resemblance to actual persons, living or dead, or actual events is purely coincidental. The opinions expressed or beliefs held are those of the characters and should not be assumed to be the opinions or beliefs of the author.

www.ingramcontent.com/pod-product-compliance
Lightning Source LLC
Chambersburg PA
CBHW030837200726
48285CB00007B/2467